THE CRUNCHBONE CASTLE CHRONICLES

PRINCE MARVIN'S GREAT MOMENT

Karen Wallace

illustrated by Helen Flook

A & C Black • London

To Helen F
with thanks

First published 2006 by
A & C Black Publishers Ltd
38 Soho Square, London, W1D 3HB

www.acblack.com

Text copyright © 2006 Karen Wallace
Illustrations copyright © 2006 Helen Flook

ISBN 0-7136-7554-3
ISBN 9-780-7136-7554-2

A CIP catalogue for this book is available from the British Library.

A & C Black uses paper produced with elemental chlorine-free
pulp, harvested from managed sustained forests.

Printed and bound in Great Britain by Bookmarque Ltd, Croydon

Chapter One

Prince Marvin lay on the ground, bent his elbows and put his hands flat in front of him. He took a deep breath, squeezed his eyes shut and tightened his muscles. Slowly he pushed himself upwards.

Thump! Prince Marvin fell back on the ground. *Whoosh*! A great gasp of air escaped from his mouth and his arms flopped like bits of wet string.

A great sob welled up in Prince Marvin's throat. Why was he so thin and weedy when his twin sister, Princess Gusty Ox, was so tough and enormous? No matter how many helpings of boiled deer and dumplings he ate, it didn't make any difference.

Prince Marvin jammed his bony knuckles into his mouth to stop himself howling. He would *never*, *ever* be a brave, bold knight!

On the other side of the green, he saw the drawbridge to Crunchbone Castle rise into the air. A moment later, his sister's deep laughter rang in his ears. Prince Marvin shook his head. Princess Gusty Ox had pulled up the drawbridge and was about to play chicken as it fell to the ground.

Now Prince Marvin sat up and watched his sister thunder across the grass as the shadow of the falling drawbridge grew in front of her. Any minute now, there would be a great *crash*! and Princess Gusty Ox would jump free. Then she would beat her chest with her meaty fists and whoop in triumph.

But the impossible happened!

Prince Marvin watched in horror as Princess Gusty Ox slipped and the drawbridge fell on top of her!

There was a muffled shout and the sound of splintering wood. Then everything went quiet. Prince Marvin struggled to his feet and ran towards the castle as fast as he could.

'You're a very naughty princess!' cried Crackle, the court wizard, five minutes later. 'Now you've broken the drawbridge and your poor father will have to pay for a new one!'

'Fluga-du-ba-thog,' muttered Princess Gusty Ox. She was sitting in a heap on the grass. Beside her, the drawbridge had cracked in two and a line of jagged timbers stuck up in the air.

Prince Marvin peered into his sister's face. There was something funny about her eyes. The pupils had turned to pin points and they were both looking inwards. 'Crackle,' he said in a worried voice. 'I think Princess Gusty Ox must have hit her head very hard.'

'Obviously,' replied Crackle. 'Look at the poor drawbridge!' He put two fingers to his mouth and whistled.

Grunt and Shovel, the king's trusty gardeners, came running from behind a nearby bush.

'Put the princess in a safe place,' ordered Crackle. He turned to Prince Marvin. 'Don't worry, she'll get better soon.'

Prince Marvin watched nervously as Grunt and Shovel heaved his sister into an enormous wheelbarrow and pushed her under the shelter of a high hedge.

A shiver passed over him. Ever since they had won their father's challenge to find a game they could play without fighting, he had grown rather fond of his sister. Of course, they still argued some days but on the whole Princess Gusty Ox had stopped hitting him over the head and he had stopped calling her names.

They got on better with their father, too. Nowadays King Cudgel was happy to let his daughter deal with any disasters that came up and carry out tasks like dragon slaying and monster hunting. And it suited the princess as much as the king.

The nervous feeling in Prince Marvin's stomach got stronger. What if a disaster happened while Princess Gusty Ox was talking gobbledygook? What if his father asked *him* to sort it out? Prince Marvin looked down at his white, skinny arms. He could feel another howl coming on.

∞

'No! No! No!' screamed King Cudgel. 'I *hate* yellow, you know that!' He raised his shrivelled parnsip nose into the air

and sniffed noisily. 'Besides, it smells of peppermints and I hate them, too.'

'That's only because you ate too many at the last ball,' muttered Quail, the king's trusty servant, under his breath. He put down the yellow velvet doublet decorated with turquoise bunnies and edged with gold lace.

All morning, Quail had been trying to help the king decide what to wear for the annual Crunchbone Castle Ball. So far King Cudgel had said no to every outfit Quail had taken out of the wardrobe.

And each time he had declared that it smelled. So, one by one, Quail had handed the clothes to Mangle, the king's laundry maid, and she had taken them outside to air them in the sun.

Quail rubbed a weary hand over his face. 'Sire,' he said, patiently. 'The ball is tomorrow night. If you want to win the best-dressed king prize again, you must make up your mind without delay.'

King Cudgel paced back and forth. On the whole, he thought of himself as an easy-going sort of king. His two children did pretty much what they wanted. And he hadn't objected when his wife, Queen Carrion, had announced she was taking up bear hunting. Although he regretted it now since that fateful day, almost a year ago, when the queen had picked up a walking stick instead of her sword and never returned from the forest.

However, when it came to the question of clothes, things were different. King Cudgel was famous throughout the kingdom as a snappy dresser. He believed it was his royal duty to look flash at all times, and that was that. In fact he believed bad dress sense was almost a crime.

Now King Cudgel looked from the window to where dozens of his outfits flapped like brightly coloured flags on the line.

Not one of them was right. And yet…

The king looked again. If there was one thing he was an expert at, it was mixing and matching. Suddenly he had a flash of inspiration!

'Quail!' he cried. 'You see the purple satin pantaloons? What if we put them with the pink—'

But he never finished his question.

A bellow of rage ripped through the air like an explosion of thunder. The next moment there was a *pop*, *pop*, *pop* sound and huge dollops of green slime dropped out of the sky and splattered the castle.

King Cudgel grabbed hold of the stone windowsill and his mouth turned into a huge quivering O.

'Sire!' cried Quail, running across the room. 'What—'

They both watched in horror as green slime ran down the castle walls and gathered in puddles on the ground. It hung from the branches of trees and covered the flowerbeds. It floated in slimy ribbons on the castle moat.

'Aaargh!' In the garden, Princess Gusty Ox was shaking green slime from her face and her hair and her arms.

A small green thing ran barking towards the castle door. It was Fluffy, King Cudgel's spaniel!

But, worst of all, the king's outfits hanging on the line were ruined. King Cudgel made a strange choking sound and slowly slumped to the floor.

Chapter Two

An hour later, King Cudgel called an emergency meeting in the Great Hall of Crunchbone Castle. Because that's where important matters were discussed and decisions taken.

The huge wooden door creaked open. Grunt and Shovel came in, dragging a wooden cart containing Princess Gusty Ox, propped up with cushions.

'Glung fug-a-dug,' said the princess when she saw Quail peering at her. 'Clusty slog-a-roo.' She smiled a wide child-like smile.

One look at his sister confirmed Prince

Marvin's worst fears. Now a disaster had happened and he was on his own.

King Cudgel shuffled into the room in his slippers. Ever since the green slime attack, he had refused to change out of his dressing gown. He had given up. Crackle could look after things. He pulled a rainbow-striped shawl around his shoulders and coughed.

It was the signal Crackle was waiting for. 'Sire, prince and princess, trusty servants all,' he said solemnly. 'We are gathered here to discuss this morning's terrible events.'

Crackle cleared his throat and fixed King Cudgel with a meaningful look. 'As we all know, this is not the first time Crunchbone Castle has been attacked with green slime. And, as we also know, the green slime has come from Harry the Hairy Green Giant who lives in the forest.'

Grunt grunted.

'Yes, Grunt?' snapped Crackle.

'Beggin' yer pardon, sir,' said Grunt. 'But I thought the great Queen Carrion had sorted out that giant for good.'

'Well, obviously she didn't,' replied Crackle rolling his eyes. 'Otherwise we wouldn't be here, would we?'

Shovel turned to Grunt. ''E's got a point there.'

'The point,' said Crackle, trying not to get cross, 'is that someone's going to have to visit the giant and find out why he's attacking us.' His voice went hollow. 'Otherwise, before we know it, this castle will be surrounded by a swamp of slime.'

King Cudgel buried his head in his hands. 'What about the Crunchbone Castle Ball?' he wailed. 'We can't have a ball in a castle covered in slime. We'll have to cancel it!'

'The Crunchbone Castle Ball will go ahead as planned,' announced Crackle in a firm voice.

A *gasp* filled the room.

Everyone was thinking the same thing.

How?

Princess Gusty Ox was in no shape to confront a hairy green giant, and even if

they did send her off, Harry wouldn't be able to understand a word she said.

Crackle pulled out an old biscuit tin from the folds of his cloak. 'The answer lies in the biscuit tin,' he said slowly, then he opened the lid and peeked inside.

Another bellow of rage exploded around the castle. There was a *pop, pop, pop* sound and a moment later green slime came through the windows and slid down the castle walls onto the floor.

The room was silent. You could have heard an elf sneeze.

King Cudgel let out such a howl that Quail hurried to his side. 'Sire!' he cried. 'What is it?'

'*Utter* despair,' sobbed King Cudgel. '*Everything* is ruined.'

Crackle knew something had to be done, and fast. He took a last peek inside the biscuit tin.

'Prince Marvin!' he cried, as sparks flew out of his pointy hat. 'Your great moment has come at last!'

Prince Marvin thought he knew what it was like to tremble all over, but he had no idea what it was like to shake like a rattle. Harry the Hairy Green Giant ate princes and princesses for *lunch*. He was also known to have the sulkiest, most vicious temper ever. All the animals in the forest kept far away from his cave. Every bone in Prince Marvin's body was shaking so hard it looked as if he was dancing.

'Bravo!' cried Crackle, who knew perfectly well that the young prince was absolutely terrified. He turned to King Cudgel. 'See, your son is so honoured to take on Harry the Hairy Green Giant that he is actually *dancing* with delight.' He bowed low. 'Sire, might I be allowed to assist the prince on his quest?'

'Are you going, too?' asked King Cudgel, stuffing a sugar lump in his mouth.

'Certainly not,' replied Crackle firmly. 'I'd just like to offer a little bit of magic.'

'No one needs magic with Harry the Hairy Green Giant,' declared King Cudgel. 'They need a great big stick like the one Queen Carrion took with her.'

'With great respect, sire,' said Crackle. 'That didn't work. We need to find a solution so you need never worry about your wardrobe again.'

The king swallowed the last of his sugar lumps. 'What do you suggest?'

Crackle waved a clenched fist in the air and said something that sounded very like *abracadabra*! He opened his fingers and handed Prince Marvin a small, brown parcel tied up with string.

'What's that?' asked King Cudgel, who liked to know everything. Especially what was inside mysterious parcels.

Crackle shook his head. 'I'm sorry, sire. It must remain secret from everyone including Prince Marvin.'

'Then how can I use it?' asked Prince Marvin, nervously. He had been hoping for something long and large, like a sword with magical giant-swatting powers.

Crackle's eyes spun. 'When the time is right, you will know,' he said with a cunning smile.

Chapter Three

It was early afternoon when Prince Marvin finally set out into the forest leading a donkey laden with presents for Harry the Hairy Green Giant.

In the end, they had convinced his father that a new approach was needed and that this time it would be a good idea to try to make friends with the giant.

The King had provided a huge sombrero to keep the rain off Harry's shoulders. Quail had found an extra-large thermos to keep his tea warm, a length of tartan cloth and a needle and thread. And Grunt and Shovel had picked six huge marrows and a giant pumpkin.

Now Prince Marvin tried to ignore the fizzy feeling in his stomach as the castle fell further behind him and the forest grew darker and darker. On the one hand, he knew that this was his chance to prove he could be a strong, brave knight. On the other, he was so frightened he felt like tying the donkey to a tree and running home. Of course, everyone would call him a sissy, but he was used to that.

In the end, he kept going. Even weedy Prince Marvin had some pride in his royal blood and the idea of going back to a swamp of green slime and his father's dreadful sulk was too terrible.

Soon the sun began to set and Prince Marvin stopped for the night. He knew he was near to the great rocky valley where Harry lived because the trees were getting twisted and scrubby and more and more vultures circled in the sky.

All night Prince Marvin had dreadful dreams. He dreamed he could feel Harry's knobbling green fingers around his neck. He dreamed the giant's great mouth was so near he could see the fur on his long, green teeth. He didn't sleep very well.

With dawn came an angry bellow which shook the leaves on the trees. Prince Marvin pulled a blanket over his head as fast as he could. Seconds later, dollops of green slime splattered the ground around him. Harry the Hairy Green Giant was very, very near.

Prince Marvin knew his great moment was about to happen and he felt terrible.

When the last drip of slime had fallen from the branches, he pulled the donkey back onto the path and walked into a huge valley. Nothing could have prepared Prince Marvin for what he saw next.

Halfway up a rocky ledge, outside a jagged cave, sat a truly enormous hairy green giant.

In front of him was a great bubbling cauldron and beside him was a row of goatskins filled with green slime. He had the meanest, most miserable look on his face and a gigantic catapult in his hand.

As soon as he saw Prince Marvin, Harry threw a stone at him. Then he lifted up the biggest goatskin bag, fitted it into the catapult and aimed it over the top of the forest at Crunchbone Castle.

'Please don't do that!' begged Prince Marvin, as he climbed nervously up to the mouth of the cave. 'I'm Prince Marvin of Crunchbone Castle. I've come to find out why you're attacking us with green slime.' His voice dropped and all the threats he had planned to make dried up in this throat. 'And if I fail, they'll call me a sissy again.'

Harry stared at the scrawny figure in front of him. He was about to pick him up and bite his head off when he changed his mind. The donkey looked tastier.

'The last person from the castle who came here tried to knock me out with a stick,' he said in an accusing voice.

'That would have been my mother,' replied Prince Marvin nervously. 'The Queen Carrion believes actions speak louder than words.'

'So where is this Queen Carrion now?'

'She didn't come back from a bear hunt.'

'Poor bear.' Harry picked up another stone and threw it at Prince Marvin's head. It whistled past his ear and landed with a crash down below.

Prince Marvin thought he was going to be sick. 'Don't get cross, Harry,' he pleaded. 'I've brought you some presents.' He undid the sacks on the donkey's back and handed over Quail's extra-large thermos. 'This is to keep your tea warm.'

Smash! The thermos followed the rock down the valley. 'I don't like tea,' snarled Harry. He watched as Prince Marvin hauled out the marrows and the pumpkin. 'And I *hate* vegetables.' He reached out a hairy hand and just like in his dream, Prince Marvin felt his knobbly fingers tighten around his neck.

'Gggg-ugggh-ggghh,' said Prince Marvin.

The fingers let go. 'What?' snarled Harry.

Prince Marvin pulled himself up over the rocks and sat down on a level with Harry's head. He knew that this might be his only chance to avoid becoming the giant's mid-morning snack. He decided to ask him straight out what was going on. 'Harry,' he said with a croak. 'Do you mind if I ask you a question?'

'What?'

'Why are you attacking the castle with green slime? Did you know that all my father's clothes are ruined and it's the Crunchbone Castle Ball tonight?'

'Why should I feel sorry for him?' muttered Harry. He rubbed at the thick, green hair that covered his arms. 'No one ever feels sorry for me.'

'I do.' Prince Marvin looked down the empty, rocky valley. 'It can't be much fun living here on your own.'

For a moment there was silence, then a great sob filled the air. Harry the Hairy Green Giant burst into tears!

'Nobody loves me!' wailed Harry. 'Even the animals run away.' He looked at Prince Marvin with red-rimmed eyes. 'They think I'm mean and miserable and terrifying.'

'You mustn't worry what people think.' Before he knew what he was doing, Prince Marvin had patted Harry's huge hairy hand. 'Everyone thinks I'm wet and weedy and I hate it. Even my sister is bigger and tougher than me.'

'At least you're not covered in green hair.' Harry wiped his nose against his arm. 'No one invites you anywhere if you're covered in green hair.'

Prince Marvin looked at Harry's miserable face. Could it be that the giant had only wanted to be asked to the ball?

And when he didn't get an invitation, he'd shown them how unhappy he was by attacking the castle with green slime?

'I'm sorry, Harry,' said Prince Marvin kindly. 'I, I mean, we, never realised—' Suddenly he had a flash of inspiration. 'Would you like to come to the Crunchbone Castle Ball tonight?'

'How can I?' wailed Harry.

Prince Marvin thought of the tartan cloth and the needle and thread still wrapped up in the sacks on the donkey's back. 'If it's clothes, you need…'

'It's not clothes,' muttered Harry. He hung his head and gulped.

Prince Marvin found his fingers clutching the small brown parcel that Crackle had given him. He pulled it out of his tunic pocket and carefully untied the string. Inside was a pair of gleaming silver scissors and a small hand mirror.

Then, just as Crackle had foretold, Prince Marvin suddenly knew what to do with them.

Chapter Four

Two hours later, after Prince Marvin had drawn pictures of a dozen different hairstyles with a stick in the ground, Harry finally made up his mind. And he didn't want his body to be covered in green hair, either.

'Are you absolutely sure?' asked Prince Marvin, seriously. 'You'll look completely different, you know.'

'Good,' replied Harry.

Prince Marvin pointed to a flat rock outside the front of the cave. 'OK. Lie there and I'll make a start.'

Snip! *Snip*! *Snip*! Prince Marvin had

never cut a single strand of hair in his life.
Now the scissors flew in his fingers.

When the prince had finished, Harry
checked his reflection in the mirror. 'It's
fantastic!' he cried. Then his face fell again.

'What's wrong?' asked Prince Marvin.
He was sure he'd done a good job.

'I'm not hairy any more,' said Harry.

'So?'

'So how can I be Harry the Hairy Green Giant if I'm not hairy?'

'Mmm.' Prince Marvin scratched his chin. 'But you like the haircut, right?'

'Right.'

'Then how about Harry the *Happy* Green Giant?'

A huge grin split Harry's face. 'I like it!' he cried. 'But…'

'But *what*?'

'The Crunchbone Castle Ball!' Harry plucked at his tatty fur cut-offs. '*What am I going to wear?*'

Prince Marvin had never, ever sewn anything before, let alone threaded a needle, but as soon as he pulled out the tartan cloth, he became a first-class tailor.

Snip! *Snip*! *Snip*! The next minute the cloth was cut into the shape of a huge flowing tunic with matching baggy trousers. And, seconds after that, it was all sewn together. Prince Marvin was as amazed as Harry. It was almost as if something *magical* was going on.

∞

Back at Crunchbone Castle, Princess Gusty Ox knew something was wrong but she wasn't quite sure what. She knew she was lying down and there were lots of pillows under her head but the thing she was lying in didn't feel like a bed. She opened her eyes and felt around. Behind her were two long wooden handles. She was lying in a wheelbarrow!

Princess Gusty Ox sat up with such a jolt, the wheelbarrow tipped over and she fell out. *Thud*! Her head hit the floor and suddenly her mind cleared. She remembered the falling drawbridge. She remembered the green slime attack. She even remembered the meeting in the Great Hall and watching her brother, Prince Marvin, shaking with terror at the thought of confronting Harry the Hairy Green Giant.

Princess Gusty Ox looked around her and realised she was in the nursery at the top of the castle. Poor Prince Marvin. Giant beating was *her* job. She yanked open the window and canonballed into the moat below. Prince Marvin needed her and he needed her *now*!

∞

The moment Prince Marvin had set off on his quest, King Cudgel had returned to bed in one of his famous sulks. As far as he was concerned, there was no hope of the green slime attacks stopping. Prince Marvin was too weedy to defeat Harry the Hairy Green Giant. The Crunchbone Castle Ball, the highlight of his year, was not going to happen.

Now Quail watched as Princess Gusty Ox fell past the window and landed with a splash in the moat. Seconds later, he saw her swim to the edge with powerful strokes and clamber out of the water.

'Where is Prince Marvin?' Princess Gusty Ox's deep voice blew in through the king's window.

Hope swelled in Quail's chest. There might still be time to defeat the giant. He turned to where the king was lying, stuffing his mouth with sugar lumps. 'Sire,' he cried. 'The Princess Gusty Ox is better!'

Moments later, the door to the king's bed chamber swung open and Princess Gusty Ox thundered into the room. 'Father!' she bellowed. 'Prince Marvin needs me!'

'Indeed he does!' cried King Cudgel who was holding up one of his bedspreads and trying it out as a cloak. 'How would you feel about a little giant beating?'

Before Princess Gusty Ox could reply, the king turned to Quail and pointed at his lime-green curtains. 'I see knickerbockers and a matching doublet, don't you?'

Quail bowed. But just as he stood on a chair to unhook the heavy velvet, Mangle appeared at the door. 'Beggin' yer pardon, sire,' she said. 'But Prince Marvin's below. Says 'e's 'ere for the ball. And there's a very tall gentleman wif 'im.'

Quail and King Cudgel exchanged looks.

'What do you mean *tall*?' asked Quail suspiciously.

'Does he look like a giant?' demanded the king.

'Hard to say, sire,' replied Mangle. ''Ee's wearing a sombero.'

King Cudgel's heart surged in his chest. 'Tell them to wait in the sitting room, Mangle. Tell them—' he paused and his eyes sparkled as if could barely speak with joy. 'Tell them we all need a little time to *change*!'

Chapter Five

'How do I look?' For the past two hours, Harry had been peering at the portraits of the king in the little sitting room. Now, even though he had stuck hundreds of shiny shells to his tunic and had made a belt out of polished bear teeth and braided eagle feathers, he was beginning to feel nervous.

'You look *fantastic*,' replied Prince Marvin. He smoothed down his own party outfit. It was the one he had worn last year, but he was delighted to see that the trousers were far too short. Maybe he was growing after all!

Suddenly there was a blast on a trumpet and the doors swung open. King Cudgel swept into the room. He looked wonderful in lime-green velvet knickerbockers and a matching doublet decorated with frilly black lace. Princess Gusty Ox stomped in behind him wearing an enormous white-and-scarlet polka-dot gown. Quail, Grunt and Shovel came next, dressed in the Crunchbone colours of purple and orange.

And at the very back was Crackle in his favourite midnight-blue cloak decorated with stars and his pointy hat with the sparkling gold band.

As King Cudgel walked up to Harry, the whole room went silent. What would the king say to the giant green slime thrower?

King Cudgel stared into Harry's huge brown eyes. Harry stared back. And in that instant they forgot their disagreement and decided they liked each other.

'Fab belt,' said King Cudgel. 'Did you braid all those feathers yourself?'

Harry nodded and went pink with pleasure.

'Father,' said Prince Marvin, quickly. 'May I introduce Harry the Happy Green Giant. I hope you don't mind, but I asked him to the ball.'

Harry bent down one knee. Suddenly he understood why he had taken such a liking to King Cudgel. They both *loved* clothes!

'Sire,' whispered Harry. 'If you don't mind my saying, I just *adore* your outfit! You look great in lime green.'

Now it was King Cudgel's turn to blush. Even though everyone knew how much he loved clothes, no one except Quail had ever paid him a compliment.

'Why, thank you,' cried King Cudgel. He beamed. 'If it hadn't been for you, I never would have chosen it.' He turned to where his son was watching nervously. 'Prince Marvin!' he cried. 'I am delighted you asked Harry to the ball!'

At that moment, the huge doors to the banqueting hall were thrown open. Everyone gasped as they looked at the magnificent feast that had been laid out on the high table.

King Cudgel clapped his hands. 'Let the Crunchbone Castle Ball begin,' he declared.

Princess Gusty Ox was so delighted, she shouted with delight. It was her favourite meal. There was roast suckling pig with custard, jelly and fried turnips and best of all, a huge pile of chocolate-coated acorns.

King Cudgel turned to Prince Marvin and held out his arm. 'After you, dear boy,' he cried. 'You have succeeded in your mission!'

Prince Marvin thought his chest would burst with happiness. He walked with his father into the hall and sat down beside him at the high table. During the feast he told them the story of how he had found Harry by his rocky cave and how the giant came to be with them that evening. By the end of the tale, there wasn't a dry eye at the table.

It was near midnight when the king's musicians began to play their final tune. It was King Cudgel's favourite dance.

Everyone joined hands and went round and round in a circle until they got so dizzy someone fell over.

That person was always Crackle and it was the signal for the dance to come to an end. Only then could they award the prize for the best-dressed king.

King Cudgel strode into the middle of the room and clapped his hands. It was the moment he'd been waiting for all night.

'Prince and princess, loyal subjects all,' cried King Cudgel. 'This ball is a very special one.' He turned to Harry and beamed. 'And as a result I have decided there shall be *two* awards tonight, one for the best-dressed king and the other for the best-dressed giant.' Now he smiled at Prince Marvin. 'There shall also be a special presentation.'

A loud round of applause turned into wild cheering. Grunt and Shovel were making so much noise that Princess Gusty Ox had to tell them to shut up.

King Cudgel held up his hand. 'As is the custom, Crackle will present the awards!'

It was Crackle's moment of glory. He reached into the folds of his cloak and took out a large, gold cube. 'I present King Cudgel with the golden sugar lump for being the best-dressed king at the Crunchbone Castle Ball!' he declared.

A look of pure joy passed over the king's face as he held the heavy cube in his hands. It was always the same. He could never quite believe it until it actually happened.

'Thank you,' he cried. 'Thank you so much.' He was just about to start a long acceptance speech, when Crackle held out his arms and a loud crack of lightning shot out of his pointy hat.

Now every eye in the room watched as the magician reached into his cloak. There was a gasp as Crackle took out what looked like two jewel-encrusted plates stuck together. 'And I present Harry with the award for being the best-dressed giant!'

It was a giant-sized compact mirror! Harry opened his mouth to say thank you, but instead he burst into tears.

For the last time that night, Crackle held out his arms. Now the crack of lightning was followed by a shower of silver sparks which settled in a halo around Prince Marvin's head. The clock struck midnight and a long gleaming shape appeared in Crackle's hands.

To everyone's amazement, King Cudgel stepped forward and took the gleaming shape from his wizard.

'Prince Marvin,' cried King Cudgel. 'Come and kneel before me!'

Prince Marvin was so shocked, he stood frozen to the spot. Luckily, Princess Gusty Ox saw the problem and shoved him with her foot.

In a dream, Prince Marvin saw the shape turn into a long golden sword. He knelt and felt the sword touch his shoulders, once on either side.

'Arise!' cried King Cudgel and, with a huge smile on his face, he kissed Prince Marvin on both cheeks and handed him the sword.

Every bone in Prince Marvin's body came alive. He leapt up in the air and let out a whoop of delight.

He couldn't believe it! He was holding his very own sword! But best of all were the words engraved on the blade: *To Prince Marvin – the bravest, boldest knight in the land*!